ZOMBIE ZERO
THE SHORT STORIES

LOVE LOST AT SEA

Zombie Zero: The Short Stories
Love Lost at Sea

ZOMBIE ZERO
THE SHORT STORIES

LOVE LOST AT SEA

J.K. NORRY

FOREWORD

In case you haven't heard, 2016 is the 'Year of the Zombie' for me. It's kind of a mixed blessing, being obsessed with the monster for so long. Now that we're pretty deep into the year, you are finally able to see what I saw when I made the decision on what to write about this year. Of course, I never planned to be called 'The Zombie Guy'; but I've heard it more than once, and it made me super happy every time. So be it.

In a world where prejudice is both legislated and scorned, it felt relevant to point out that every monster began as a person. Somewhere along the way, life sunk its teeth into their soul and discharged a healthy amount of venom. That venom changes people, as surely as being bitten by a zombie. And yet, they are still people. They look like us, talk like us and eat the same food.

Well, zombies start out as people too. Not only that, they are as convinced that they have as much of a right to exist and feed their hunger as the rest of us. On top of all that, they are on a mission.

Their collective hive mind is bent on a shared objective, and to them that objective is everything. As far as many of these monsters are concerned, the deeper meaning of their existence trumps the deeper meaning of humanity's. Without shame or fear or hesitation, these creatures go after what they want; and they won't stop until the world is theirs.

If you have read 'Zombie Zero: The First Zombie', then you understand all of this already. If you haven't, that's fine with me if it's fine with you. Each of these stories stands alone, even as they tie in to each other. The three stories in this book are tightly woven together, and that collective story stands on its own as well. If you're just here for some short stories, read on. If you are curious as to what order the books are meant to be read in, there are three other books you'll want to have read at this point.

'Zombie Zero: The First Zombie' is where it all began. Read that, then the first two short story volumes. They are 'The Sickness Spreads' and 'The Beginning of the End'. You can then consider yourself all caught up. If you already are caught up, thank you! I hope you are loving this ride. I sure am.

ABOUT THE SHORT STORIES

There are a couple of things you should know before you read any further. First, these sections between the stories are not going to contain any spoilers; also, you don't have to read them if you don't want to.

These sections are a chance for me to tell you a little more about what fun it was to write these stories, and how grateful I am that it is the 'Year of the Zombie'.

I'll also tell you what chapter each story ties into in 'Zombie Zero: The First Zombie', by number. If you just want the stories, feel free to skip these sections. They are for readers like me, folks who like a little back story from the author.

If you're not one of those people, it won't bother me at all if you jump right to the stories. Look for the title pages, and read from there.

There are some things I'd like to share with the rest of you. By the time I had started this set of short stories, I was pretty deep into the project. Nine other stories had been started, eight of them had been finished.

There was a good flow going with the writing, all the stories were outlined, and I was confidently headed towards slightly early completion of all eighteen stories.

Halfway through is not a good place to get cocky, it turns out. This set brought its own special challenges with it, and in many ways it was like starting at square one again. I was just beginning to realize that the order I was writing these in was not the best order to release them in, either to newsletter subscribers or in this format. That meant I had to figure that proper order out, and right in the midst of the emotional storm that this set brought with it.

'Love Lost at Sea' was instrumental in the decision to make these into six sets of three when we compiled them. It was the perfect small collection, a great way to show how this zombie revolution has more to offer than gore and brain munching. Now that you've seen the gore, and even a little of that brain munching, it's a great time to show you the softer side of the zombie apocalypse. Followed, of course, by more gore.

It's also a great time to talk about the cover artist we used for these books. The cover for 'Love Lost at Sea' is one of my favorite book covers ever; I'd like to tell you why.

ODE TO SEAN HARRINGTON

Do you know how much I love the covers for these books? When I first saw them, I asked the artist if we could make prints of the original art and sell them along with my books online and at festivals. There was a little fear there, that he might be insulted or angry that I had an additional idea after we had come up with our initial agreement.

There was also hope, that he would think that it was a great idea and would be happy that I had asked. With his customary online tendency to not mince words, Sean Harrington gave me just the answer I was hoping for. Hooray!

We started to order the prints as the art showed up, and went looking for frames as soon as they came in. We also wanted copies of our own, and as we got them we framed them and hung them in our living room. It was a cool way to watch the 'Year of the Zombie' take beautiful shape as time went on while decorating our house with fantastic original art at the same time. Each time a new piece arrived, I would totally flip out.

Then I'd message telling him how incredible it was and why I thought so. With this piece, as with all of the others, it was too easy.

Science fiction and horror pulp publications played a serious role in my literary upbringing. I gobbled them up like a zombie with a bowl full of warm brains, and I loved the cover art as much as the stories inside. When I saw this piece, I had a dozen pleasant flashbacks to precisely that time in my life. If ever there was a book cool enough to carry around in your back pocket, it's one that has a cover like this.

I can say that confidently, since this is so much like the books I carried around during those long summers full of short stories. It was a special thing to come up with the stories, made more special by Sean as we watched this art roll in.

Sean Harrington made the world of 'Zombie Zero' brilliantly visual, coming up with all of these short story collection covers on his own. There are not enough words to tell you or him how happy I am that it was his mind and his hands at work on this project. I'll keep trying, though.

Thanks, Sean! Every cover is my favorite, for a different reason! This one is quite simply perfectly perfect.

ODE TO DAWN MARSHALL

A weird thing can happen when you get really close with someone, or at least it has happened to me: it gets easy to use words like 'I' and 'we' interchangeably, and assume that everyone just knows what you mean. There comes a time when a little explaining is in order, lest folks think I'm even stranger than I actually am.

I have a partner in publishing, and her name is Dawn Marshall. She's also my partner in pretty much everything else, which is a big part of why life is so good for me. See, Dawn takes special care in everything she does; it's truly a blessing to have such a committed and dedicated partner, and to watch my books take shape under her direction.

My idea of formatting is a strange one, as is my vision of graphic design and typesetting. In my world, I ask for what I want according to what I see in my head. Then Dawn delivers, and one of three things happens:

The first possibility is that it's perfect, we both love it, and we move on to the next aspect or stage of the project together.

That's always nice; and the more we do what we do, the more often it happens.The second possibility is that it's just what I asked for... unfortunately it's also awful, and we come up with something different.

The third is a more complicated possibility that happens just as often as the other two: Dawn shows me something different than what I asked for, I say that isn't what I asked for, she shows me the version that was what I asked for, and I admit that her idea is way better. Then I breathe a huge sigh of relief, glad once again to be part of such a great company and wonderful partnership.

It's vindicating, in a weird way. I know what it's like to have the best idea in the room. It's not as great as it's cracked up to be, and confidence in a good idea is easily seen as arrogance through the wrong eyes. The only time it's truly gratifying is when someone else has the next best idea, and the creative mind gets a chance to both praise another creative mind and breathe for a minute. I owe Dawn a continual debt of gratitude for making the Sudden Insight Publishing offices my favorite place to have a meeting. Since we both work from home, I also get to be continually grateful to her to making it my favorite place I've ever lived.

ABOUT KIRSTEN'S DREAM

There is another set of short stories coming that takes place partially on the ocean, 'Volume V: Monstrous Consequences'. It's no coincidence, of course; the open seas look pretty inviting when flesh-eating monsters are covering the land. I mention the other set of short stories because they were actually the set I had been working on right before this one. That seemed a little problematic, to me.

This whole thing isn't about people on boats during the zombie apocalypse, and I didn't want it to seem like it was headed in that direction. Releasing two short stories to subscribers sequentially featuring folks on boats would feel like that's where we were going, and I didn't want that. I certainly didn't want the two book sets to come out one after the other, and that was one of the many considerations we weighed when setting up release dates.

That meant I had to stay on schedule with writing at this point; my wiggle room was suddenly gone. That was no problem; the schedule had suited me fine until then.

With nine stories started and eight done, I started on 'Kirsten's Dream' tenth. In putting off wrapping up one story that I knew would end in an upsetting death, I dove headfirst into this one. Or should I say 'heart first'?

One thing anyone who knows me or my writing knows about me is that I have no shame about crying. When I am happy or uplifted or touched or sad, I cry. You can call me sappy or sensitive or whatever else you want; the days of fighting my nature are behind me, and I'm neither especially proud nor particularly ashamed to be an emotional person. I just am. I use it as a guidance system, and it serves me well. Then, every once in a while, I meet someone like Kirsten.

Right away, I liked this young lady. I related to her in a number of ways, and delighted in seeing the world through her eyes. When the story really started taking shape, that's when those tears really started to flow. It was like the salty ocean was leaking out through my eyes as I wrote this story that I loved so much. I've seen bottles of writer's tears for sale on the internet.

Those are totally real, you know.

This story, like the next one, ties in to the beginning of Chapter 16 in 'Zombie Zero: The First Zombie'. I hope you love it!

KIRSTEN'S DREAM

Kirsten had never wanted a perfect family. She knew kids with perfect families; she found them boring. She had never wanted to be popular, and she had never found a boy or a girl that made her want to act silly or scream a name from a mountaintop. All Kirsten ever really wanted was to grow up, and know what the world was like from a place of power instead of a position of helplessness. That dream had never seemed ridiculous; everybody grew up eventually. Now her dream had been taken from her; it would be buried in the ground along with her youthful body, and neither would ever see maturity.

It wasn't the best idea, running away like she had. The doctors said she could live longer if she took it easy, and if she let them keep a close eye on her. They wanted her to avoid anything that might set her heart to racing: strenuous physical activity, severe emotional upset, exciting situations. All the things that teenagers indulged in regularly were suddenly off limits to Kirsten; she had cried out dramatically to the doctor that he wanted her to avoid life. He had not disagreed.

It wasn't the worst idea, either; running away like she had. It would give her parents a chance to mourn her missing rather than endure her presence. They were not a happy couple under normal circumstances, nor were they particularly well off. The extra stress of a fourteen year old daughter with a heart just waiting to explode had put even more strain on their relationship, and their finances. It was better that she was gone.

Besides, her decision had been locked in; there was no going back now. If Kirsten had decided to break into a house or sleep on the streets, she may have found herself regretting her decision and retracing her steps. Instead she had gone down to the marina, dove into the water and swam around the gated entrance. Pulling herself up onto the dock, Kirsten had gone from one giant boat to the next. Finally she had found a key taped to a doorframe and let herself into a spacious cabin. She had raided the fridge, watched a movie and sipped at some liquor. Somehow she had ended up in a storage locker, wrapped in blankets and the sweet drunken fog of sleep.

The vessel had gotten underway while she slept, and by the time she woke up they were far out to sea. Kirsten had spent a day vomiting quietly into a blanket, wrapping it around itself again and again until it was a wet dripping mess, and listening to voices too muffled to understand. She dozed and threw up sporadically throughout the day, until the booze or the seasickness worked its way through her system. A rhythmic thumping woke her, at some point, and Kirsten's heart raced; it sounded like someone was pounding on the door to her little cubby. One of the voices started up again, getting louder as the pounding came faster; they were the first words she had been able to understand, and they made her flush.

Finally the pounding and the loud crying out stopped, all at once, and the voices grew even quieter than before. Kirsten waited another twenty minutes in the following silence, then crept out into the cabin. It was dark, but she remembered the layout; she went immediately to the refrigerator. Gulping at the fresh taste of chilled bottled flavorlessness, Kirsten swished a mouthful around while she groped for the sink. She spit in it when she found it, repeated the cleansing process and spit again.

For a moment she thought of lifting her bottom into the sink; she had to go to the bathroom something fierce. Her questing hand had brushed dishes and silver in the basin; she didn't want to pee on their dirty dinner dishes, or poke herself with a steak knife. The bathroom was right next to the bedroom; she had availed herself of its availability earlier, when she had been poking around. She would wake them up if she used it now, and risk being chased around the boat by two startled nude adults. Better to creep out on deck and hang her butt over the side.

It was nicer than Kirsten had expected, full night over the ocean. She couldn't see lights in any direction but up, which set her heart racing when she first realized it; then she focused on those lights, the distant stars and the hovering moon, and the triphammer in her chest went back to an irregular slow broken clock rhythm once more. Kirsten stayed out on deck all night, wondering which way home was and what the word really meant. Was home the place she had left behind? Was it the place she was going to? Was it awaiting her on the other side of the final beats of her runaway pulse? Or was it here, under the stars in the middle of nowhere?

Before it got light out, Kirsten grabbed a couple slices of bread and ham from the fridge, tossed her sodden vomit-laden blanket overboard, and hid herself once again in the storage compartment. She promised herself that she would tell them tomorrow, find a good time and announce her trespass. It wouldn't do for them to find her crashed on their sofa, or sprawled on their deck. Kirsten nestled even further into the closet, moving all of the supplies quietly closer to the door and pulling all the blankets back into the depths of the space with her.

It wasn't long after she got comfortable that she heard activity in the cabin. She was tired, but the thought of another stiff sleep in the closet didn't appeal to her nearly as much as the possibility that they might offer up their bed. When she heard two distinct voices, Kirsten girded herself for the confrontation; then she heard that thump on the door, softer than last night but just as steady, and saved the thought for after a nap.

* * *

Kirsten went out on deck when she woke up; she could see them swimming below.

She didn't want them to be frightened, or startled, climbing onto their boat to find her waiting for them. She watched them swim for awhile, swiped a little more food from the kitchen, and snuggled up in the storage compartment before they could make it aboard again. It wasn't really so bad in there, and she seemed to be catching up on her sleep. Telling them could wait until tomorrow, after another night spent under the stars while they slept.

For three days and three nights she told herself that; on the fourth Kirsten realized that the only way they were going to find out was if they found her. It was too awkward at this point, with how many times they had made love close to her hiding spot; and after so many days, she fell into a routine to mirror theirs. Kirsten seemed to enjoy her quiet starry nights as much as they enjoyed celebrating their togetherness throughout the day; of course, she was much more careful about not waking them up. Still she felt like she was on vacation, alone, and it crossed her mind more than once that she would never grow up to take a vacation of her own. If she told them, they would turn the boat around for sure; Kirsten didn't want that. She wanted more quiet starry nights.

Hanging her bottom over the side of the boat had become routine, but it was nice when they went swimming or snorkeling. Kirsten even got their lazy schedule down well enough to take a couple of showers; she felt bad taking fresh clothes, and tossing hers overboard. It didn't stop her from doing it, of course; but she did feel bad about it.

Then one evening their voices grew loud, in alarm rather than pleasure, and Kirsten didn't need to strain to hear their words.

"They're not hailing us," one voice said.

"They're coming right for us," answered the other.

"What kind of flag is that?" the first voice asked.

"I don't know," the other cried out. "It must be pirates, or..."

"You don't think..." the other voice spoke again.

"I'm not going to think that," the first replied, "and neither are you. Come on, I have a couple pistols. Let's go out on deck."

They were the last words she heard clearly; after that it was muffled shouting, followed by gunfire. Then it was screaming, horrible screaming that seemed to last forever. When it was cut off, and silence ensued, Kirsten hugged her knees to her chest and tried to calm her heart. Tears streamed down her cheeks, and the little storage compartment seemed to be closing in around her.

She heard footsteps in the cabin, and Kirsten tried to hold her breath. Her heart just pounded harder in her chest, and she had to gasp in a lungful of air to make up for having held it. For a moment she thought the footsteps were moving closer; then they went away, and she heard a horrific cry come from the upper deck. It was answered by a dozen more, what sounded like hungry animals baying in chorus. The sound was like nothing she had ever heard before, and it sent chills up Kirsten's spine. It kept up, long loud hungry howls that drifted away as the other vessel did.

When she was sure she was alone in the cabin, Kirsten slowly opened the door to the little storage compartment. She went into the bathroom and vomited in the toilet until it felt like she might turn inside out if she retched any more. Flushing, she wondered if maybe it was going the same place it had when she hung her butt over the side. There was no need to be quick about taking a shower, or finding a new outfit to wear. At this point it wasn't even stealing, or so she assumed. Kirsten hadn't the courage to wander around on deck looking for recognizable body parts; she did have whatever it took to claim the bed, and she lay sprawled on it for a long while before deciding she could maybe eat something.

Stepping from the bedroom, Kirsten froze. Someone was already raiding the fridge. As he turned, she screamed. He dropped an armful of food, spreading his hands defenselessly before him.

"It's okay," he said. "I'm not going to hurt you. I only-"

Kirsten screamed again.

He clapped his hands over his ears, shouted over her piercing wail.

"Please stop screaming!" he cried. "I'm not going to hurt you!"

Kirsten stopped screaming, took a deep breath to start up again. Her heart was pounding in her chest, and suddenly she couldn't breathe. Grasping at the air, she felt her eyes go wide as the world began to go dark. She lurched toward him, tumbled into his grasp.

He caught her, lifted her easily in his arms. He carried her into the bedroom while he talked, set her gently on the comforter.

"I'm going to lay you down," he said

quietly. "You need to calm down. I'm not going to hurt you. My name's Nick. Let's get you settled now, that's it. Just relax. There's nothing to worry about any more. You'll feel all better in a minute, then we'll talk. I'm going to go get you some water, okay?"

The world was coming back into focus, but her heart was still pounding. She watched her racing thoughts; it was like watching a car speed by, only to realize it had been her driving it. Except that Kirsten would never drive a car.

He continued talking to her from the cabin, to ease her mind or his. His calm measured tone helped her focus, gave her something slow to set the tempo of her heart to. Kirsten latched onto it, a steady anchor for the drifting ship of her runaway brain.

"Everything is going to be all right," he called out softly. "I'm sorry your folks are gone, but I'll take care of you. I hope you didn't have to see what happened. I know it's a lot to take in, what's happened to the world, but we're really lucky to be where we are."

Nick stepped back into the room, held out an uncapped bottle of water. He helped her sit up, and held her torso upright while she drank.

Kirsten's heart was not going to burst. Not this time, anyway. She sipped at the water, calmed her breathing.

"What do you mean?" she wheezed. "What's happened to the world?"

He looked at her funny for a long quiet moment, until Kirsten started to squirm under his gaze. Finally he shook his head, looked away.

"Nothing," he murmured. "What's your name?"

"Kirsten," she said. "Nick, right?"

She stuck her little hand out, like her dad had taught her to, and gave his a good squeeze when he took it. He grinned.

"Yeah," he said. "Nice to meet you, Kirsten. Are you feeling better?"

"Uh-huh." She nodded, flushed. "I just got too worked up."

Nick waved his big hand dismissively.

"It happens to the best of us," he said. "Often at the worst of times."

"No," Kirsten scooted toward him. "I can't..."

She looked up at him, standing beside the bed. For the first time, she realized that he was handsome. Handsome, and grown up. Like she would never be. She sighed. There was no reason to tell him her life story, short as it may be.

"Yeah, you're right," she said instead.

Standing shakily, Kirsten fought the urge to smile as he reached out for her; he was only trying to help. She brushed his hand away, moved into the main cabin. Nick trailed her, watching her every move carefully until she settled on the sofa. He glanced at the kitchen space.

"You're not hungry, are you?" he asked. "I know you just lost your folks, and I don't mean to be rude, but I haven't eaten anything decent in..."

He trailed off, and Nick's eyes went somewhere that looked like it caused him pain to visit.

"Promise me something," Kirsten said, quietly.

"If I can," Nick shrugged. He glanced at the refrigerator.

"Promise you won't make me go anywhere I don't want to go."

For another minute, Nick gave her that weird look again. He nodded, in understanding or inner resolution, and echoed her sentiment.

"Kirsten, I promise I will never try to make you go anywhere that you don't want to go," he said, solemnly. "This is your boat, no matter the circumstances by which it came into your possession, and I am grateful to you for saving my life. This boat goes where you say, when you say, Captain Kirsten."

She beamed. "Well, in that case I should tell you a couple things. First, those were not my folks. They were super nice, or they seemed to be, but they weren't my family. Second..."

Kirsten trailed off as his gaze drifted to the kitchen again.

"Second," she repeated, putting it off until a little later. "I'm starving. Let's have us a proper meal, shall we?"

His shoulders sagged in relief, and Nick turned abruptly.

"I'll get it," he said. "You take it easy, talk to me."

"Yeah?" Kirsten watched him nod as he moved to pick up the items he had dropped, and wash off the packaging before setting them on the counter. He dried them with a hand towel, glancing at her as he unwrapped the food.

"All right," she smiled. "Where are you from?"

Nick laughed, opened a drawer and pulled out a knife for chopping.

"That's not talking, that's getting me to

talk," he pointed out. "I'm too hungry to talk. Where are you from?"

Kirsten hesitated, and Nick stopped what he was doing. He turned to her.

"I promised," he said. "I don't break promises."

"No matter what?" Kirsten asked meekly.

Nick nodded. "No matter what."

He held her eyes, to show he was serious. Kirsten felt her heart start to pound. She nodded, gave him a weak smile.

"Okay," she said.

Nick went back to preparing a meal, and Kirsten paused while thinking of where to start.

"Well," she said. "I'm from San Francisco. I found out that I was sick a few weeks ago, and I couldn't take the way everyone was treating me. So I ran away. I was going to sleep on the nicest boat in the marina for a couple nights, then probably go home, but..."

Nick turned, washed his hands and dried them while he looked at her.

"Kirsten," he said. "How old are you?"

"Nick-"

"I promised," he said again, firmly.

"Fourteen," she blurted. "I'm fourteen years old."

"Really?" He shook his head, turned his back. "I thought you were sixteen, at least fifteen. Were your folks...okay?"

Kirsten laughed. "I suppose you could say that. That, and nothing more. My folks were mediocre in every way. Me being alive was a huge strain on them before they found out. Afterwards, it was like they had found out I was an alien or something. They were scared to talk to me, or touch me."

Flushing, she rushed to explain.

"Not that I have anything contagious or anything," she said, quickly. "They just didn't know how to deal with me. I wanted them to get on with their lives, and ignoring me like they had before, but they wouldn't let me be. It was the same as being in the hospital, someone coming in every five minutes to wake me up and tell me I needed to get some rest. It was driving me crazy."

His back still to her as he set something to sizzling on the stovetop, Nick called quietly over his shoulder.

"So," he said. "Can I ask?"

"What?" Kirsten asked. "What's wrong with me? It's a heart thing. My pulse won't settle on a regular rhythm, and sometimes it gets going too fast and won't slow down. Someday it won't stop beating faster and faster, and my little ticker will stop going tock for good."

They were both quiet for a minute, him cooking and her thinking, before she thought to add something.

"Some day very soon," she said. "I won't ever grow up."

Nick stopped moving, his back still to her. The warm wonderful smells of breakfast filled the air, and the sounds of sizzling.

"That's too young," he said, and stirred the potatoes. He shook his head. "That's too damned young to be facing death every day."

He turned, and there were tears in his eyes.

"I'm sorry, Kirsten," he said, shaking his head. "I'm so sorry."

"Why?" Kirsten sat up, glanced past him. "Did you burn my breakfast?"

Nick looked at her, a puzzled expression on his face. After a minute, he nodded. He had made another promise, without saying it, and Kirsten understood: no more death talk, unless she wanted it. She sighed with relief as he brought her breakfast over to her, and grinned.

"Sorry," he said. "I only burned it a little."

Kirsten took her plate, set it on the little coffee table that was affixed to the floor.

Looking up at Nick, she raised an eyebrow.

"Should we sit at the table?" she asked.

Nick shrugged. "It's your boat, Captain."

Giggling, Kirsten patted the cushion next to her.

"Well then, have a seat," she said. "First mate."

Kirsten picked up the remote control, pointed it at the television.

"Want to watch something?" she asked.

Nick's eyes went wide, and his fork stopped short of shoveling a heaping pile of potatoes into his mouth.

"Is there reception on this boat?" he asked.

Kirsten nodded. "There's a DVD player too."

"Anything worth watching?" Nick asked. "Not horror, please."

Giggling again, Kirsten hopped to her feet and opened the cabinet. She threw out a few options, and Nick finally made a face that didn't make him look like what he was eating tasted terrible. Kirsten popped in the disc, and settled in to watch it with him. She fell asleep after eating, and leaned into him. Kirsten woke up once with her head against his arm, and a while later in bed alone. She could hear his loud snoring from the other room, and the low rhythm of it lulled her back to sleep.

*　*　*

They spent the next day cleaning the blood off the deck, and fishing for rock fish or ling cod. Something got caught on the line once, but it was big and the line snapped. Nick cursed the people who had bought the boat for not having better gear until Kirsten started to imitate his rants. They swam around the boat, sunned themselves on the deck and watched a couple more movies. He treated her like a person, instead of a kid, and they talked about how life had been for both of them. Kirsten got so caught up in enjoying his company, and his cooking, she nearly missed the obvious. She paused the movie after another great dinner to thank him, and ask him outright.

"Nick," she said. "What is it that you're not telling me?"

He shrugged. "What do you mean?"

"Come on," she nudged him. "You haven't treated me like I was a dumb kid all day. Please don't start now. I know you're a good guy. You must have people that you love, that love you back. Plus, you wouldn't ordinarily hang out with a fourteen year old girl on a boat alone. You would try to get me back to my folks, or at least try to get in touch with yours. What gives, First Mate?"

"Aw, hell," Nick said. He deflated. "You're not going to believe me."

Kirsten shook her head. "Yes I will."

"All right." Nick shrugged, looked her dead in the eye. "You asked for it. There's been some kind of outbreak. Some people are calling it a zombie virus. Everyone agrees on one thing: the infected are eating people. My family and friends are dead. Yours probably are too."

She felt her eyes grow wider as he spoke, and her heart began to pound in her chest. Kirsten thought of her parents, the kids and teachers at her school, her neighbors. She looked at him, questions without words.

"Do you want to see the news?" he asked, picking up the remote. Kirsten shook her head, tried to calm her breathing.

"Kirsten?" A worried look clouded his face. "Are you alright?"

The look cleared, and his countenance was suddenly a study in panic.

"Oh, Kirsten! I'm so sorry!" He stood, wrung his hands. "I forgot all about your... your heart. Oh, I'm such a jackass. I'm sorry."

Her heart slowed, and she gathered enough air to laugh at him.

"Calm down," she said, patting the sofa. "I'll be okay."

She breathed, and he watched her, until she turned to him and spoke again.

"Nick," she murmured. "What happened to you?"

He smiled, sadly. For a few moments, Nick stared into the distance of his recent past. Then he spoke, quietly.

"I was in the navy," he said. "Our vessel was docked, it was my first night on a new assignment. I don't know how they got on board; I was asleep when it happened. When I woke up there was someone eating the guy that had been sleeping next to me. I got the hell out of there, hid in the engine room, and slowly started to starve to death. The heat in the engine room made it so they couldn't see my heat signature through the walls, but it made it a hard place to hide out. The noise was tremendous, and it was driving me crazy. I kept looking for a chance to board another vessel, and finally the opportunity presented itself."

"What are they doing at sea?" she asked. "They can drive a ship?"

Nick nodded. "They can pilot ships and

subs; they're not animals. They hunt like animals, they feed like animals, but they think like people. There's another vessel accompanying the warship I was on, a submarine from a different nation's navy. They're scouring the ocean for survivors. Big ships are being boarded, and overcome by the submarine, as the crew and passengers focus on the approaching warship. They sink the ships if they don't feel like overtaking them. They leave the small ones to drift, empty."

"Like this one," Kirsten breathed.

"Like this one," Nick echoed.

She shook her head. "How did you get away?"

"One of them helped me," Nick said, shaking his head. "It was all kind of a blur, after I don't know how long in that hot noisy room."

Kirsten nodded, and made note of the pain in his eyes. She picked up the remote off the coffee table, and put the movie back into motion. No wonder he hadn't wanted to watch horror; Nick had just lived through it.

* * *

Nick knew how to drive the boat

wherever she wanted, and that's just what he offered to do. For the next several days they chased schools of fish and fading sunsets, talked about the way the world used to be and watched nearly every movie in the cabinet. They avoided the news, the shore and their obviously dwindling food supplies. Nick never told her how much fuel they were using, but Kirsten knew the tank wasn't getting any fuller. She wanted to tell him to take over, to assume her role as captain and find a safe place for them to go. It was possible that he was doing all this to give her control of what life she had left; but it was also possible that there was no place to go, and he knew it. If she asked him to take her somewhere safe, she would find out the truth.

So she didn't ask. She swam and sunned with him, explored the endless ocean with him, and began to drop hints. When they ran out of movies that he hadn't said no to, she suggested they watch the news. He had told her that maybe it was time for him to give chick flicks a chance. When they ate she would leave some on her plate, complain of being full and ask if he wanted any more. It always took some coaxing, but he never left a bite when the convincing was over. After several such instances, he finally refused. He paused the movie they were watching and turned to her on the sofa.

"I know what you're doing," he said, clearly displeased.

Kirsten shrugged. "I might say the same about you."

Nick screwed up his face, trying to look angry. It would have been terrifying the first time she saw him, if he had glared at her that way. Now she knew him, though, and that he would never hurt her. She sensed the ability to do violence within him, surely, but not against her. Kirsten had to fight the urge to laugh.

Still scowling, Nick asked, "What do you mean?"

Kirsten shrugged again, resisting a smile. "You first."

"You're not eating all your food because you want me to eat it," he said. "You're not full; you're trying to be nice."

She let the laugh come at last.

"And you," she poked him, frowning playfully, "You're giving me as much food as you give yourself. That's ridiculous. If this is the right amount of food for me, then it's not enough for you. You're twice my size, Nick. You've got all those big muscles to feed. And besides, I'm..."

"You're what?" he demanded.

Now it seemed like he was a little angry, and she realized why. They hadn't talked about her condition, or the state of the world, for days. Kirsten was breaking their agreement by bringing it up, shattering the illusion of the fragile world they had built together. She placed her hand on his, gently.

"I'm dying," she said quietly. She waved off his protestations with the hand that wasn't holding his. "You're not. You've been very kind, letting me decide where to go and insisting I sleep in the bed and stuffing me full of delicious food. But if you keep putting me first, you aren't going to last. It would be a horrible thing for a man like you to die because you were too kind to think of yourself. You need to get somewhere with food, and water, and people. Whoever is left needs people like you to help them. You and I are both being selfish by indulging my dying wish. We can't do this anymore."

Nick deflated while she spoke, but he wouldn't agree with her.

"You want me to let you starve?" he demanded.

"No," Kirsten shook her head. "I want you to ration us both according to our bodyweight and order of importance. Isn't that what you would have done in this situation in the navy?"

"We're not in the navy, Kirsten," he sighed. "And there's very little chance of me surviving if I go back. You don't understand what is going on. My choices have been narrowed to being eaten alive from the inside by starvation and being eaten alive from the outside by zombies. I'll take starvation any day. Besides, I've been catching more fish lately. This is not an unsustainable situation."

"Liar," she frowned. "We're going to run out of drinking water, and fuel at some point. We'll die of thirst even if fish jump onto the boat all day. Besides, how do you know how bad it is out there? Maybe they've gotten a handle on the situation."

Nick shook his head doggedly. "They haven't," he said. "I've been watching the news after you go to sleep. Every nation has fallen, and they've taken over the networks that haven't gone dark."

"They?" Kirsten's eyes went wide. "You mean the..."

Nick nodded.

She grabbed at the remote, to change the feed on the television. Nick was faster; he grabbed her hand, held it gently but firmly, and shook his head. Kirsten pulled away, angry.

"Let me see," she said.

"All right," Nick nodded. "Calm down first, though, okay? You're already mad at me, and it's a shocking sight for anyone."

"Let's have a drink," Kirsten said, nodding.

Her eyes went to the little liquor cabinet, as she had seen his do quite a few times over the past week. Nick frowned at her.

"Finish your dinner first please," he said.

Kirsten leaned forward, shoveled half of her remaining pasta onto his plate. She smiled at him disarmingly.

"I'll split it with you," she offered.

They ate the last few bites together in silence, then Nick stood to get them fresh glasses and a bottle.

"Any preference?" he asked.

"Is there anything in there that was bottled before I was born?"

He laughed. "Yeah, some port and some scotch."

"Mmm," she grinned. "Port, then."

Nick gave her a funny look, and Kirsten laughed at him.

"I'm from California," she giggled. "They teach us about wine in elementary school.

If we're drinking port, you should put those glasses back and grab those little tiny wine glasses. Those are for port."

"Well, la-de-da," he chuckled, returning to the sofa with tiny glasses in one hand and a bottle in the other. He worked the wax free of the opening, pulled the cork and poured a bit in each glass. Kirsten laughed, leaned forward and grabbed the bottle. Nick made as it to protest, until she filled his glass and left her own half full. Setting the bottle down again, she held up her little glass.

"Bodyweight rations," she said, by way of explanation. "Salut."

Nick laughed. "Cheers," he said.

They clinked, and drank. Nick poured another half glass for her, filled his own, and picked up the remote. He waited until she had taken a sip, watching her.

Kirsten furrowed her brow. "Is it that bad?"

"It's worse," he murmured, draining his drink.

He switched the feed, and Kirsten gasped despite herself.

Nick changed the channel, immediately, and suddenly she was watching monsters in suits reporting the news. It was still shocking, but not nearly as bad as what they had just seen. Kirsten listened to them talk about the dwindling supply of fresh human flesh, and give other monsters suggestions on where to hunt, before she spoke.

"What was that other channel?" she asked, shuddering.

"It's a show about a pack of zombies hunting a human," he frowned. "They show it every night. The human never gets away. They play cat and mouse for an hour and then eat the person alive."

"For an hour?" Kirsten whispered.

"Yeah," he said. "Sometimes longer. They don't seem to care if their shows run long, and there's no advertising. It still doesn't make it worth watching."

"You do, though," Kirsten noted. "How come?"

Nick shrugged. "Looking for a weakness, or some sign of hope, or wishing just one victim would escape."

"Maybe they do," Kirsten pointed out. "Maybe those episodes don't air. You don't actually think reality television is real, do you?"

He laughed. "That's a nice thought, anyway."

Kirsten hushed him, leaned into the lighted screen to listen to the news anchor.

"There's good news, of course," he said. "Anyone who dies in the remote places we can't reach will become one of us. The sanctuary housing them will be ours as soon as they do, and it won't be long now. Folks are getting sick, and running out of food and water. Soon the doors of the most concealed safe houses and bunkers will be opened from within, and we will be there when they do. The boats on the water will-"

Nick shut off the broadcast.

"Hey!" Kirsten punched him, lightly. "I was watching that."

"You saw enough," he said, firmly.

"I saw enough to know that I'm going to turn into a monster when I die, and that I'm apparently going to try to eat you," Kirsten huffed. "I'd say I need to know a little more."

Nick sighed heavily. "Like what?"

"Like what?" Kirsten fluttered her hands in the air between them. "Like, is there any way to prevent me from becoming a zombie? Is there any way to make sure you survive my death?"

He shook his head. "Calm down, Kirsten. Please."

"I'm not going to calm down, Nick," she sputtered. "I'm about to become a freaking monster! Did you see that thing? Those teeth? Those eyes? That's going to be me soon! Calm down?!"

Cursing herself inside for her habit of not cursing in front of adults, Kirsten glared at him to show him that she was serious nonetheless.

"There are two stages," Nick said, evenly. "The bitten and the dead turn into what they are calling 'ramblers'. They are slow, but strong. At the first taste of human flesh, they begin to transform into what you saw on the broadcast. They call those 'howlers'."

Kirsten remembered the sounds she had heard as the other vessel had drifted away, the hungry baying of a hundred animals. She shuddered.

"Do you know how to stop it?" she asked. "Is there any way to prevent me from becoming a...a rambler?"

Nick looked away. "No."

Grasping his hand, Kirsten made him meet her gaze.

"You're lying," she said.

Nick nodded. "I'm not cutting off your head, Kirsten."

"Do you have a gun?" she asked.

It looked like he was thinking of lying to her again; then he shook his head, and answered honestly.

"Yeah," he said. "I have a gun."

"Would that work?"

Nick shuddered, shook his head. "It should, yeah. But I couldn't-"

"You couldn't what?" Kirsten demanded, angry again. "Grant a dying girl her last wish? Prevent my transformation into a monster? What, Nick? You couldn't what?"

She saw tears shining in his eyes, but Kirsten wouldn't let up. She leapt to her feet, spoke down at him.

"You have to promise me," she said firmly. "You have to promise that you'll put a couple bullets in my brain; and if that doesn't work, you have to promise to cut off my head. You have to, Nick, or I'm going out on deck and jumping overboard right now. I'll cut myself, so the sharks will smell my blood in the water. If you don't stop me from trying to eat you, then I'll stop myself. Right freaking now."

Nick mirrored her stern look, though tears still stood out in his eyes. While she stood there, trembling and swaying a little, he spoke.

"Sit down," he said. "Please."

Kirsten took a step.

"What if they find a cure?" he said behind her. "I could never forgive myself. You can't ask me to do this."

"A cure?" Kirsten whirled on him. "I'll be dead, Nick. A cure would only bring me back into a human body that can no longer sustain life. I might be upset, but you're the one not thinking clearly."

She turned her back on him, took another step.

"I promise," he said, quietly.

Kirsten stopped. "What?"

"I said I promise," Nick answered, louder. "Please sit down. Finish the movie with me. Let's not talk about this any more."

They had almost two days together after that. It was a sweet honest kind of freedom that they shared during that time, and Kirsten forgot all her new habits and boundaries. She swam and screamed and splashed in the water with him, spent too much time in the sun, and drank a lot less of the dwindling water supply than she pretended to. She was in the shower, with the water nearly scalding her skin as it washed away the salt and sweat, when her heart began racing.

She knew right away; this was it. Kirsten groped for a towel, gasping for breath, as her vision narrowed to a tiny speck. Fumbling at the door handle, she collapsed against the thin barrier as she finally turned the knob.

Naked, the towel tangling itself about her knees, Kirsten collapsed into the main cabin. Nick rushed to her side, lifted her in his arms and carried her to the bed. He covered her in a thin blanket, to hide her undeveloped body from view. She smiled as he leaned in, touched his face.

"Thank you, Nick," she whispered. "You made my dream come true."

"Hush," he said, patting her wet hair. "You're going to be fine. Just relax. Catch your breath."

Kirsten shook her head, smiled again.

"Not this time," she murmured. She touched his cheek again. Her next words were barely audible, even to her.

"You promised," she said.

Nick nodded. "I did."

A tear slipped from his eye to wet her thumb. Kirsten smiled one last time, let her hand fall to her side, and closed her eyes.

Nick took her pulse, wiped his tears with his forearm, and went to the storage closet. He removed the pistol he had stashed there, went back into the bedroom and put two bullets into what used to be Kirsten's brain. He watched her body for about twenty minutes, then carried her out on deck and tossed her over the side. Returning to the cabin, ignoring the tears that flowed freely down his face, Nick took a bottle from the liquor cabinet and went back out on deck with it. He poured a little over the side, let loose with a wretched sob that sloshed more whiskey in the water, and set about to drinking the rest.

When he woke on deck a few hours later, shivering, Nick put his hand to his throbbing head. He drank what was left in the bottle with the other hand, then stood and retched violently over the side of the boat. He returned to the cabin, closed the door to the little bedroom that smelled like her sleep, and passed out on the sofa.

ABOUT CHELSEA'S CRY

Did you like 'Kirsten's Dream'? I hope so. Now you see why it kind of wrecked me emotionally. There were a few days after completing it where I felt like I should be wearing a black armband so folks knew how I felt inside. This marked almost the exact halfway point in all of the 'Year of the Zombie' projects I had planned, and it was not the first time I had seriously considered that I had really set myself up for some serious emotional upheaval with all of this zombie business.

What do you get when you cross an author who gets very attached to their characters with an apocalypse? A lot of tears, it turns out. I don't always get to know the end of the stories I'm writing, and I never get all the details upfront; but it's kind of obvious that a lot of people are going to die in a story about the end of the world.

It's a good thing I didn't consider that seriously until the first big hit in the 'Zombie Zero: The First Zombie'; I won't tell you who it was, just that it wasn't easy.

Having considered it several more times at this point, I considered it once more after writing that last story. It was relatively easy to go back and end the life I had left hanging, and wrap up the story I had left undone, although even that was not without its own liquid salty sadness. Alright, I admit it: I'm a little sappy.

So there I was, on the other side of halfway done. Momentum had become a natural thing at this point, and it seems only appropriate that momentum is almost a character in this next story. It carried me right out of the dull melancholy that I found myself left with after Kirsten's story. I'm not just a little sappy, I'm also a bit of a romantic. I love a good love story, although I prefer the ones that serve a higher purpose and have a deeper meaning.

Naturally, that is just what I have to offer you next. Don't let the lovey stuff fool you; this is definitely a monster story. Confronted with a choice between romance and terror, Chelsea came along to show me that there was no need to choose: I could have both! This story brought me up and dropped me down, heart-wise, only to bring me up again. I hope you enjoy 'Chelsea's Cry'. Technically, it actually starts at the beginning of Chapter 16 of 'Zombie Zero: The First Zombie'.

CHELSEA'S CRY

"You think you failed them." Chelsea frowned, shook her head. "But what more could you have done?"

"I could have stayed, Chelsea."

"You would have died," Chelsea answered. "We would have both died. Is that what you wanted?"

"Of course not. But I'm a senator. I have responsibilities. I made commitments to my constituents."

"You're also a woman," Chelsea answered. "And my wife. You made commitments to me too."

Denise nodded, took her in her arms. Chelsea rested her head on Denise's shoulder, nuzzled her neck and breathed in her scent.

"I know," Denise said. "That's why we're here, instead of back there. I looked over my contract and saw no mention of any 'zombie outbreak' requirements. They told us, but they gave us nowhere to go; they just said get out of the city, away from people."

Chelsea nodded, her nose tracing

Denise's jawline.

"So here we are," Chelsea murmured. "All alone on the open sea, with nothing to do and nowhere to go but further away from people."

She pulled away a little, while staying in the orbit of Denise's warm embrace. Chelsea leaned in, kissed her.

"Who knew the end of the world could be so nice?" Chelsea murmured, smiling. She couldn't see Denise frowning, the way Chelsea was nuzzling her; but she could feel it in the stiffness of their embrace.

Despite the tone of their exchange, they were not on the aft deck. Chelsea and Denise embraced with the future filling their view and the past behind them. It was the way they had always lived their lives, first separately and now together. Chelsea did not worry about losing her to 'could have beens'; the present moment was far too appealing to Denise's optimistic paradigm.

Sure enough, Chelsea felt the senator pull her closer; she felt Denise's lips find hers again, as her arms wound about her more tightly. Chelsea lost herself in her scent, her flavor, her kiss. Soon they were pressed together in every way they could be, making out like school kids while the ocean opened up before them. By all appearances, they were a couple in love on a happy vacation.

After awhile, Chelsea felt a chill run up her spine. The ocean air was growing cooler, and they hadn't eaten in their haste to escape the city. She stepped back, smiled coyly at Denise and led her into the cabin.

"Do you want me to take you in the kitchen or the bedroom?" she asked, still holding Denise's hand as they entered the warmth and quiet.

"I'm always hungry for you," Denise squeezed her hand. "But I am feeling a little woozy. Of course, it could be your intoxicating kisses."

Chelsea opened the full size refrigerator, scanned its contents.

"Want some burritos?" she asked. "Or pasta?"

"Okay." Denise moved toward the sofa, her attention clearly not on her own response. "Sounds great."

"Sweetheart," Chelsea murmured quietly. "What sounds great?"

"Dinner." Denise waved her hand dismissively. She leaned to pick up the television remote. "You know. Whatever you said."

"Denise." Chelsea's voice was even

quieter than before. It had been a sweet lesson for her, after having raised her voice so many times to be heard so little: Denise tuned out voices raised in argumentative tones dripping with bluster; she zeroed in on the calm soft sound of reason.

Denise stopped reaching for the controller, stood up straight to give Chelsea her full attention.

"What's the matter, babe?"

Chelsea shrugged. "Can we not have the television on?"

"I just wanted to watch the news."

"I know." Chelsea turned from the kitchenette, crossed the floor to take her hand. "I know you want to watch the news; but I don't. I hate the news, I always have. I knew that keeping up on it was a part of your job, before. But you've been let go, sweetheart. The world doesn't need you anymore. The news doesn't need you anymore. It's all over, baby. The only person that needs you now is me."

"And you hate the news." Denise said flatly.

Chelsea nodded, flushed.

"I would've been happy to have taken that secret to my grave," she said. "I would have been even happier to tell you when we were much older, and you had left politics behind. I imagined us laughing about it, sitting in rocking chairs on our front porch sipping tea."

"Aww," Denise sat on the sofa, pulled Chelsea to sit down next to her. "So you do still love the idea of us growing old together?"

Chelsea nodded. "Well, yeah. My hair will be more blue than yours, of course, but otherwise we'll be virtually indistinguishable for all the wrinkles and time spent together."

"But you hate the news?"

Chelsea rolled her eyes.

"It's so sensationalized," she shrugged. "And it's always bad; or at least most of the time. The most terrible stuff happening in a really beautiful world. Why not report eighty percent good stuff, or ninety-nine? Good things happen every day too. Why isn't that what gets reported on? If they had a show about the good news, I might watch it and enjoy myself; but I hate the bad news. It's like a constant horrific advertisement for the worst among us. They should at least be honest, and call it that. It's not 'the news', it's 'the bad news'. And the only reason there's so much of it to report is because there are more of us than ever before. The world is actually safer, statistically, than it was twenty years ago, or ever in history; but the numbers are so high, the news has enough examples to make it look like we're all sadistic savages."

She was breathing fast, and talking fast too. Denise was smiling, watching her get worked up and being openly amused by it.

"You've really been holding this in, haven't you?" she asked, still smiling. "You know that the population is not expected to survive this current news event, right?"

"I do," Chelsea nodded. "I still see no reason to watch the worst of it happen. Once again, it will be all the horrible moments that get the most viewership. The beautiful moments will be ignored, lost forever like they always were, in the stinky soup of what people like to watch happen to other people."

"Anything else?" Denise was still smiling.

"What do you mean?"

Denise shrugged. "Are there any other secrets you were keeping from me, things you can tell me now that the world is ending?"

Chelsea frowned in the most attractive manner she could, stared off into nothing as if thinking of something.

"No..." she murmured, "not that..."

"Hmm..." Chelsea said, trying not to giggle. She made her frown look as fierce as she could.

"Oh!" Chelsea's eyes went wide, as if she was remembering something. "Your dad is ruthless asshole."

Denise laughed.

"That's no secret," she said. "You really haven't been paying attention to the news, have you?"

Sticking out her tongue playfully, Chelsea stood.

"Please?" she asked. "No news?"

Denise sighed, nodded. "All right. No news."

Chelsea returned to the kitchen area, threw a glance over her shoulder.

"So?" she said. "Burritos or pasta?"

"Ooh, pasta," Denise smiled. "We should have a bottle of wine to go with that. What do you think?"

Opening the refrigerator again, Chelsea nodded.

"I think that sounds wonderful," she answered.

They cooked, and talked, and drank almost the entire bottle of wine together. There were a few moments where they both forgot what they had left behind, and they were sweet moments. Then they remembered, together, and talked about all the people they had known and loved. After awhile their soft words led to tender touching, and then the tenderness gave way to an urgency. They needed to be close, in every way they could, in all the ways words fell short.

Chelsea found herself pleasantly pressed up against the counter, with her clothes in a concentric pattern on the floor where Denise had dropped them piece by piece. One of her legs was over Denise's shoulder, the other dangling off the counter. She cried out pleasured broken words, describing what Denise was doing and how much it was driving her happily crazy to feel her doing it. In every other moment Denise's touch was delightfully overwhelming, and Chelsea's dangling leg twitched with the pleasure. Chelsea's heel struck the door to the storage cabinet under the counter with the regularity of a ticking clock, the thuds punctuated by her ecstatic cries.

They talked together afterwards, holding each other close and murmuring words that only had meaning to them. Their kisses were tender deliciousness, their touches light with exhaustion. It took all their remaining strength to find their way to the bedroom, and collapse on the mattress together. They slept in each other's arms, lost in a world that wasn't ending, peaceful.

* * *

That first day set the tone for the rest of their days. Chelsea woke up before Denise the first day, fixed her breakfast in bed and then took her dessert in the kitchen. It was the reverse scenario of the night before, Chelsea pushing her up on the counter to toss one of Denise's ankles over her shoulder to hear her love cry out her own pleasure. Chelsea went on deck after and stripped nude, then dove into the water; she swam around the boat until Denise joined her, and they both nearly drowned trying to make love in the ocean.

Laughing and gasping for air, they went back to the cabin and talked and watched old movies they had already seen. The day flew by, and they smiled and laughed like they perhaps never had. They didn't talk about the state of the world, and they didn't watch any news. There was no attempt to reconnect with the world, and no desire to; this was their forever vacation, and they were fully present in every sweet moment of it. They were both aware that they would run out of food before long, and fresh water; it was a conversation that they waited to have until they needed to have it. Then another conversation was interrupted, as the world came to them, and the food discussion never had to happen.

They were sitting in the cabin, talking about their respective childhoods, when Chelsea put her hand on Denise's.

"Sweetie," she said. "What I said about your dad...I'm sorry."

Denise laughed quietly.

"You were joking," she said, "and you weren't wrong."

"Maybe," Chelsea shrugged. "I'm still sorry. I know you still loved him, and that he's probably..."

"What?" Denise laughed again. "Locked in a posh shelter with my mom and a dozen other ruthless assholes? You don't think he's dead, do you? I mean, he probably will be eventually, but he'll be one of the last to go. There are a lot of lives that he is willing to lay down before it comes time to lose his own. Babe, who do you think called me?"

"Did he tell you where they were going?"

"No." Denise shook her head. "Only that

there wasn't room for us."

"What?" Chelsea sat up straighter, narrowed her eyes. "There wasn't room for you, or there wasn't room for us?"

Denise sighed. "It doesn't matter."

Chelsea opened her mouth, ready to say something; then she stopped, and stood up. Crossing the cabin, she pressed her hands against the glass.

"There's a ship out there," she breathed. "A big ship."

Denise moved to stand beside her; they watched the approaching vessel in silence for a full minute. When Denise spoke, her voice was loud and strained; though Chelsea stood right next to her, her voice went up in volume and pitch as well when she responded.

"They're not hailing us," Denise cried.

"They're coming right for us," Chelsea responded, clutching her hand.

"What kind of flag is that?" Denise's voice cracked with the strain.

Chelsea looked at the flapping fabric; the picture was almost cartoonish, terrifying in its stark bloody detail. It looked like a picture of a monster, a creature with a face full of teeth and a mouth full of blood.

"I don't know," Chelsea cried. "It must

be pirates, or…"

She looked from the window to her wife, squeezed her hand again. Frowning, fighting back tears, Chelsea spoke again.

"You don't think…" she asked.

"I'm not going to think that," Denise replied, "and neither are you. Come on, I have a couple pistols. Let's go out on deck."

The guns were hidden well, but easy to access; it was only a half a minute before they were on deck, hailing the giant ship.

"Hey!" Denise waved her arms in wide arcs, the pistol tucked into her waistband at her back. She smiled, although there was no one on the deck of the other vessel as far as they could see.

"You're headed right for us!" she cried. "Divert your course or state your reasons for approaching!"

The ship kept drifting toward them; it seemed to be slowing, but it was not changing course.

Chelsea turned to her. "Should we try to outrun it?"

Denise shook her head.

"No," she said. "It's a military vessel, sweetheart. They could take us out at any time, and overtake us with zero difficulty. We need to find out what they want."

A door was open, a slab of steel slid aside to reveal nothing but a darkened passageway. The square of space bobbed ten or fifteen feet over the calm smooth surface of the water; they could see it as the ship drew ever closer. It had nearly come to a stop beside them when the first monster poked his head out of the hole.

Chelsea screamed, and the creature grinned at her. His mouth was full of jagged teeth, ragged rows of razor sharpness that chomped at the empty air in hungry anticipation. He leapt across the space between the vessels, grasping the side of their boat with long talons that ripped gashes in the deck as he pulled himself the rest of the way aboard. Another monster leapt over him, planting a foot on his head to land only feet from them. Chelsea screamed again, while Denise stepped forward.

In one fluid movement, Denise swung the pistol around and shot the creature in one rusted red eye. The bright orb became a burst of blood, and he fell twitching to the deck. In time with his fall, Denise fired at the monster behind him. Just as he got his feet under him on the deck, the bullet took him full in the forehead. He slammed backward onto the deck, rolled and stood again in one shocking second. The next shot took him in the eye, and he went down beside the other.

Chelsea realized she was still screaming, and that Denise was drawing a bead on another monster set to leap from ship to boat. She silenced herself, drew the pistol Denise had given her, and aimed with a trembling hand. Both pistols fired at once; the creature shook off the bullet that buried itself in its shoulder, then craned its neck to see where the other had gone. There was a small dent in the hull, several feet from him, where Chelsea's shaky shot had struck. He howled, and leapt to their deck.

The rest of Denise's clip went into his face and chest; then his teeth sank into her shoulder, and they went down on the deck together. Now Denise screamed, and Chelsea began rapidly firing point blank at the monster. The first two shots turned his head, and the third found his eye. He collapsed on top of Denise, just as her eyes fluttered and closed.

"No!" Chelsea cried.

She stepped forward, toward the two that had boarded during the scuffle. Seven more shots rang out, peppering the monsters about their faces with the rest of her bullets. The dull click of her pulling the trigger with no round was lost in her scream as what used to be Denise clamped her teeth about Chelsea's ankle. It was more than just the pain of the bite, or the realization of the betrayal as she looked down, that made her cry out: a searing pain started at the bite, shooting its way up her leg to invade every cell of her body. Chelsea's cry began as a terrified scream and ended in a strangled growl. Her eyes closed, and she fell unconscious to the deck.

* * *

When Chelsea's eyes opened, they had changed from a brilliant blue to a rusted red. Her flesh was hanging from her face in ungainly clumps, and the palms of her hands left a skin-colored smear on the deck where she placed them to lift herself up. A horrible hunger twisted her insides, and her thoughts were a muddled murky mess of cobwebs in her aching head. She blinked, watching part of one of her eyelids fall off, then shook her head to clear her vision. It was shadow and light all mixed into a confusing mess, colors screaming like colors had never screamed at her. After a full minute of adjusting to her new paradigm, Chelsea finally grasped what was happening.

The monster that had its back to her wasn't a monster; it was her wife. The creatures it was warding off were the monsters; they were trying to get around her, or through her, to get to Chelsea.

They wanted to eat her.

Chelsea moaned, clumsily tottered to her feet. Dragging herself the few steps that were between them, she came to stand beside Denise. She moaned again.

Denise turned to her and smiled. She had dozens of teeth now, though her skull was not the rigid armored helmet that characterized the others. Still slim and shapely like a human, Denise turned back to the monsters. She howled softly, gestured at Chelsea.

The other creatures turned their backs, some in obvious disgust; Denise led her to the edge of the deck, trailing them. One of them stepped around them, and Denise held her protectively close as he passed; while he investigated the empty cabin, Denise threw Chelsea over her shoulder and leapt aboard the ship. A minute later the last monster boarded behind them, and shut the sliding steel panel.

There was no calling out, no message

shouted or radioed in; nonetheless, the ship began moving the moment the door closed. Denise nearly lost her footing, leaning into Chelsea and tossing them both against vertical steel. She collected them both, then led Chelsea by the hand from one section of the ship to the next. Howlers stood in hungry clumps and watched them, whispering or howling their hunger after they had passed. They found barracks, with bunks, but they were wide open spaces that would be difficult to defend. Several of the sheets were stained with blood, dried and gone stiff; the smell of it hung in the air, and twisted her belly with hunger.

Finally they found a storage cubby, a place they could rest and go unnoticed. Denise collapsed as soon as the door was secured behind them, and Chelsea rushed to her side at a hurried scuffle. She knelt, and held her arm in front of Denise's mouth where it had fallen open. Denise blinked, looked at the arm, and licked her lips. Her rusted red eyes went to Chelsea's.

"Hungry," Chelsea moaned. "Eat."

Denise bit what was left of her own lip, shook her head.

"No," she growled. "Not yet. Rest."

She wrapped her fingers carefully about

Chelsea's arm. Her nails were only a little longer than before, but they were sharp and jagged. If they cut her, Denise would surely be unable to resist that temptation of the flesh. The smell of it would drive her mad, as mad as it had made them both begin to feel in the barracks, and she would consume Chelsea within minutes. Chelsea felt her tender touch as she was pulled into Denise's embrace. They spooned together on the floor, amidst neatly stacked rations that would never get eaten, and fought their hunger.

It seemed like days, but it was only a couple of hours before Denise sat up; she grinned malevolently, showing Chelsea her rows of baby zombie teeth. She patted Chelsea on the shoulder as she got up, and went to the door; she bounced in place while turning the handle, her hunger turning to anticipation as she fumbled with the mechanism. Before slipping through, and closing it behind her, Denise put one finger to her lips and smiled at her again.

"Wait here," she growled. "I'll be back."

They were barely words, but Chelsea understood. She waited, trembling with fear and twitching with hunger. It was a mindless wait, as if what little thought she'd had had slipped out with Denise. Time passed, with no numbers in her head to count it by and no memories in her mind to look over for the hundredth time. Chelsea sat, waiting and twitching, until the door opened once more.

The head that poked into the room was like the others she had seen; hairless and horrific, the skin had dripped from her face to reveal the new sinew that had grown in its place. A ridge along the top of her skull anchored the slabs of muscle to further empower her jagged rows of teeth. She was taller, her limbs lengthened freakishly and her torso reshaped around her armored ribcage. Her face and front were covered in blood, and stringy chunks of fatty tissue were caught between her teeth. At first Chelsea feared she had been discovered, and began the slow awkward struggle of trying to stand up; then the monster stepped into the room, and she let her weight drop to the floor once more.

It was something in her eyes, or her walk, or her smile; though they were all different than before, they were all still Denise somehow. The last part of her to slip through the doorway was her taloned hand, and it was holding something.

Chelsea sat forward, sniffed at the sudden

overwhelming odor. It was fresh flesh, nearly an entire arm that had been torn or bitten off. Blood still dripped from the place where a body had once been attached to it, and Chelsea moaned as precious droplets struck the floor. Leaning further froward, she put her dead weight on her hands and began crawling toward it. She left bloody smears with swirls of flesh coloring everywhere her hands touched the floor. When she got to Denise, she stayed on all fours while she began to devour the flesh.

It was still warm, and delightfully full of blood. Denise held it while she tore strips of flesh from the bone and licked dribbling red droplets from her own chin. Chelsea felt new teeth coming in, pushing out the old ineffective flat ones. They shredded the flesh in her mouth, pressing it insistently against the back of her throat until she swallowed and took another bite. It wasn't long before the arm was nothing but dangling bones, and Chelsea was on her way to becoming a proper monster. She felt stronger, and faster, as did her gnawing hunger; she stood easily, looked up at Denise.

A picture flooded her mind, as clear as the image on a television screen. It showed dozens of people, hundreds of them, running from howlers in panicked confusion. Most of them were carrying more flesh than they needed, and for the first time Chelsea found the common feature an attractive one. Somehow she knew that this was where Denise had just been, and that it was Denise's thought in her head. She asked questions without forming words, wondering silently aloud in the spacious chamber of her starving thoughtlessness.

Is it over? She looked the question at Denise. Are there more?

When Denise took her hand this time, it was with more urgency than gentleness. Chelsea felt long sharp talons slicing the skin that had not fallen away on its own, and she clenched her own hand tightly about the pain. Her blood flowed, for a moment, then the wounds closed around the razored slashers; they moved through the doorway, merged in spirit and flesh and hunger.

Chelsea felt the twisting in her belly, the gnawing need that had grown exponentially with those few precious mouthfuls of flesh. She hungered for more, hot wet splashing bites against her face; but more than that, she hungered for the change. It was clear that Denise could run on ahead, cover every square inch of the ship before Chelsea could drag her partially transformed body up on deck. It was nice to be faster, and stronger, and to have her body not twitching spastically every time the thought of flesh entered her mind; but the hunger was everything, screaming in her every cell and exhausting her new power as it flowed.

She felt Denise's mind reach out to hers again, was grateful for the image and its message. Chelsea collapsed in the hallway, waved her on and stayed with her somehow as she dashed away. Through Denise's beautiful rusted red eyes she watched, delighting in the power and speed and purpose of her every savage motion. She moved like an animal, without thoughts of limits or pain. Denise allowed her thoughts to fall away, and let her hunger become the power in her limbs and the reason for the run. On all fours, she cleared flights of stairs by leaping from one landing to the next; following her consuming need, she burst out on deck and into the open night air.

It was nearly empty, and Denise did not pause on the steel surface. She continued moving, so fast that she crossed the deck in moments and was suddenly aloft in the cool night air. She looked down as she began to descend, and Chelsea saw the other ship through her hungry eyes. The deck was wooden, and lower than theirs; but not by much. Her leap had been more to get a better view than to cross the space between the ships; when Denise's feet hit the deck, she streaked immediately in the direction of a dozen glowing heat signatures. Chelsea could smell their fear, and their flesh, and their desperation; she drooled mindlessly, leaning bodily against the wall, tasting the blood and skin in Denise's mouth as she took down a screaming mound of flesh.

She tore off both of his arms while chomping at his shoulder; rather than scream, or protest, he let the first change wash over him. Lying there in a growing puddle of his own blood, his skin gone gray and already beginning to hang loose from his face, he rocked back and forth helplessly without arms. His belly prevented him from sitting up all the way, and he couldn't seem to leverage his own weight without hands. Rolling around, he offered up his leg as Denise turned away. She ignored the offering. Chelsea watched her retrace her steps, and in less than a minute they were feasting together.

With a belly full of flesh, Chelsea leapt to her feet and howled. She felt the power coursing through her veins, the hardening of her skull, the rows of teeth in her mouth growing longer and more numerous. From within, she felt the change trying to use the fuel to armor her ribcage and move her organs behind them. The arm had not been enough, and the hunger twisted at her insides again as she stood. She followed Denise, watching the way she mentally kept track of Chelsea without ever turning around. She stayed two steps ahead, slowing when Chelsea was weakened by her hunger and picking up speed when it drove her urgently forward. It took them longer to reach the deck than it had taken Denise by herself, but soon they stood in the open night air together.

The space between the vessels looked further through Chelsea's eyes than it had through Denise's. Hesitating at the railing, Chelsea watched the heat signatures moving on deck; she listened to the sweet swan song of men and women running and screaming and dying. She glanced at Denise, then at the wide gap between one deck and the other. Denise nodded, understanding. She took Chelsea's clawed digits in hers, and leaned over to brush her monstrous lack of lips against Chelsea's heavy skull; then she let go of her hand.

Denise backed up a few steps; smiling at Chelsea, she blurred past her and launched herself into the air. Chelsea watched, smiling, as she sailed smoothly over the gap and hit the deck running. Most of the people out in the open were being eaten or had already transformed. Several ramblers dragged their feet past her, looking to eat or be eaten; Denise ignored them. She disappeared into a doorway, and Chelsea switched to watching her through Denise's eyes as she tracked down a frightened heat signature. Chelsea watched her corner a woman, and saw the woman collapse in unconscious panic before Denise could lay a lethal hand on her. Denise caught her mid-fall, threw her over one monstrous shoulder, and carried the woman out on deck.

Switching to her own eyes, Chelsea saw Denise appear through the same doorway she had entered moments ago. She watched her dash forward, stop abruptly at the railing and heave. She howled as the woman arced through the air, and her howl was punctuated by the dull wet sound of the woman's body striking the deck a few feet from where Chelsea waited. She was upon the body before it stopped rolling, biting at the first part of her that she came upon.

The woman opened her eyes as most of her foot disappeared into Chelsea's toothy maw. She screamed, and the sound burst forth to delight Chelsea's ears while blood exploded to fill her mouth. She crunched at the bones, slurped at the hot wetness, and ground the woman's toes into a delicious paste. Swallowing, Chelsea moved her head to the woman's ankle; by the time she had eaten her achilles tendon, and most of her calf, the woman was shoving her own flesh insistently into Chelsea's mouth. It was like trying to find a rhythm with an inexperienced and overly eager lover, and the woman's leg pushed her around on the deck while Chelsea ate.

Annoyed with the movements, Chelsea let the leg drop to the deck. She moved to the woman's neck, and ate what little muscle was there in three quick bites. The fourth went through her spine, and the woman's lifeless head rolled away as Chelsea spit out the mouthful of hard bone and crushed powder. She went back to eating the body, rolling the still corpse onto its stomach so she could ravage her meaty buttocks and thighs. It tasted different, dead flesh, and she hungered for more fresh bursts of blood while gnawing at the cooling corpse. As if someone in the sky were listening to her thoughts, another heat signature hit the deck beside her. He was screaming, and trying to stand; he struggled with a broken leg while he watched her approach, dragging himself painfully away from her hunger.

Chelsea abandoned the dead flesh, leapt on the living. She had been so overwhelmed by the pleasure of slaking her hunger momentarily, Chelsea had not noticed the transformation completing itself within her. Her limbs had grown longer, more powerful; her body and mind were perfectly shaped for destruction, and she overtook her prey with ridiculous ease. She ate his shoulders, then his arms and legs; when she was done with him, he was a gray-faced torso twitching in a huge puddle of his own blood. Chelsea was caked in gore, and her face and hands were painted in solid sheets of sticky red wetness.

Rising to her feet, Chelsea reached out to her wife in her mind. She saw Denise's talons tearing apart a family, tasted the flesh that filled her mouth, and let out a long hungry howl. Without backing up, or getting a running start, Chelsea leapt high into the air. Throwing out her powerful arms, stretching her talons wide, she let the wind whistle through her fingers as gravity dragged her downward. She landed on the wooded deck of the other ship, moved to the closest doorway. Switching between her own eyes and Denise's, Chelsea found her way to the guest cabin where Denise was feasting.

The door was already a splintered mess, and she shouldered the hanging remains aside to enter the room. From the looks of it, there had been three of four members to this family before Denise had discovered them. Now it was all blood and strips of flesh, staining the floor and walls around the final dwindling family member. Denise was eating what appeared to be a man; it was hard to tell, with his face and arms gone and the rest of him drenched in blood. Chelsea dropped to all fours to join her, and within a few minutes nothing but blood remained.

Moving up the hallway, staring through doors in search of heat and fear pulsing on the other side, they both stopped as the floor lurched under their feet. They exchanged a look, but no words: the ship was moving. They shrugged, together, and went back to their search. A few more doorways were dark and quiet, as they passed; soon they heard and smelled blood. For the next couple hours they ravaged one cabin after another, tore a single or a couple or a family to pieces with their teeth and talons. They went into the inner cabins as the sun began to rise, to get away from the glare. The smell of blood hung in the air, but the flesh smell had gone from fresh fear to dead decay while they had feasted.

Other howlers began to crowd the small inner cabins, piling on top of each other to form writhing masses of bloodied bodies so deep that beds were lost in the tangle. Chelsea and Denise watched one room after another fill with monstrous piles of zombies; when they got settled in, despite elbows in their faces and other bodies on top of them, each howler drifted into a guiltless animal slumber. Envious of the peaceful blanket of unconsciousness that seemed to be weaving its way through the ship, neither of them wanted to climb onto a bunch of strangers and sleep. They wanted to be in each other's arms, alone.

Denise tugged at her hand, leading Chelsea back out on deck. It wasn't a main deck; there was no view, for all the hanging lifeboats. Denise climbed into one of them, motioned for Chelsea. She caught the scent after Denise, as she ascended the ladder; Denise held a finger to her lipless mouth, shushing her. As Chelsea brought her body over the top of the ladder to peer into the lifeboat, she saw the source of the smell. Denise was standing over the couple where they huddled against an inner wall together, daring them to scream or move with her bold stance. They held each other, trembling and giving off the most delicious scent of fear.

Moving to stand beside her, Chelsea imitated Denise's confident stance. She stood over them while Denise showed her a picture of her intention and then vacated the space to make it happen. A few moments after she disappeared, a whirring noise began, and the little boat dropped. The couple gasped, together, and held each other closer; a menacing look from Chelsea silenced them. The little enclosed space continued to move slowly under their feet, descending to the water below. When they hit, the distant whir stopped; Denise's feet struck the hull a moment later. She climbed into the open chamber, went to a lever mounted to the wall and leaned forward to inspect it. Carefully, she pulled a small metal pin from its place, then yanked the handle downward.

The little vessel lurched under their feet again, in all directions at once. Denise wrapped Chelsea in her arms as she staggered past, and held her firmly to her monstrous body. Taking her hand, she led her to the front of the bobbing lifeboat. She showed her the controls, fired up the engine, and flashed a picture of the vessel cutting a clear path across the water and away from the looming ship. Chelsea watched the sea through the windshield, and watched Denise tend to the living breathing flesh through her wife's eyes.

Denise bound their hands, tied them together and tied one of their legs off tight just above the knee. She grasped just under the tourniquet and about the ankle, and pulled. They were a ways off from the ship now, and Chelsea turned to look questions at her. Denise shot her a mental image, two rotting ramblers feeding them until they found more flesh. Then she shot her another image of the people, both alive but limbless; they could supply their need for days, if it came to that.

Nodding, Chelsea knelt beside her to nibble on the meaty calf with her wife. She loved how Denise always thought ahead, and always thought of her; after licking the blood from the bones, cracking them and sucking out the marrow, she leaned into the new embrace of Denise's long and powerful arms. She licked a trail of blood from the part of her face that used to be her cheek, and they laughed together. After awhile, Denise rose to string a blanket across the thick pane of glass, to block out the sun; there were rations in the cubby with the blankets, and she threw them at the flesh's feet. She brought another blanket over, lowered herself beside Chelsea again and wrapped them both in its warmth.

Chelsea felt her wife against her skin, smelled the flesh and blood for tomorrow, and snuggled deeper into her monstrous embrace. She fell asleep with a toothy smile on her face and a bloody tear on what used to be her cheek. Denise waited until her breathing came calm and slow and even; she threw one last glance at the shocked flesh, closed her eyes and followed Chelsea into sleep. In their dreams they were together, like they had always been; like it was supposed to be.

ABOUT NICK'S MISSION

Do you hear that? Is it a happy holler? A fearful shout? A hungry howl? No, it's Chelsea's cry! Wasn't that sweet? And kind of gory, too? And fun! I sure thought so. It's nice to know that even howlers have a softer side; well...some of them, anyway.

That was one of my favorite themes in all of this, how some turned monster and still held on to some shred of their humanity. It's not surprising that love is what ignites such memories and desires; it is the only motivator more powerful than need, after all.

We've come to the last story in the book, and I hope you're excited to read it. You remember Nick, from Kirsten's story? Well, this is about his mission, and how it keeps on changing. We've all got to have a mission to keep us motivated, and sometimes that mission has to be altered or even scrapped altogether as life and times change. In a world where ups and downs are often considered some sort of even keel, I hate to think of how hard it would be if everything that makes life so easy began to crumble.

Of course there would be people that fell, people that gave up, people that tried and failed, and people who never bothered to try at all. From what I've heard, the end of the world is never particularly discriminating; it's happy to take nearly everyone. Those left behind are left to wonder if maybe the early victims were the lucky ones after all.

Well, I guess we're done with the sweet stuff. Talk about taking things to a dark place.

Geez, Jay; way to kill a mood.

Sometimes answering one question leads to another, and so it was with this story. I had to know how this all came together, so I poked around the magic portal in my head with a particular question in mind. Always ready to be sent away, I was delighted to see the window light up with just the scene I had been wanting to see. This was one of the few stories that really shifted at the last minute, and it was a shift I was very glad to see. But you should read it first, then I'll tell you more about that.

I will tell you where to look for the tie-in to 'Zombie Zero: The First Zombie'. It's in the Epilogue, right there in the first italicized paragraph. You might want to read it afterward, though; it actually is a moment that happens after this next story ends.

NICK'S MISSION

Nick rolled over in his bunk, put his pillow over his head to block out the noise. He'd only just drifted off; or had he been asleep for hours? It was hard for him to tell. The sleep pulled at him, from above or below, and his thoughts stretched meaninglessly in that direction. The sound was pulling him in that other direction, the one full of exhaustion and soreness; he didn't want to go in that direction, though. He wanted to fall into those arms of weightlessness and not slip from their embrace for a good long while.

That sound wouldn't stop, and his mind was trying to wrap itself around it. Nick turned from the attempt, pressed the pillow tighter against his skull, fought to keep his thoughts in that vague floating place and away from words and names and definitions. The sound burrowed through the pillow, slipped through his ears and marched straight into his brain. It was wet, and rhythmic, and urgent.

The words snapped him awake. Nick lay

there, frozen, his pillow still pressed to his head. If there had been two people sharing the bunk room with him, he would have assumed they were having sex. Good sex, too, from the sounds of it; there was a lot of wet in the sound, and a great deal of urgency to the rhythm. He knew there was only one other person in the space, however; and Nick didn't like the thought of him making that much sound of that nature by himself. Disgusted, he lifted the pillow and turned his head. His mouth was open, to say something cutting; Nick closed it when he saw the actual source of the sound.

They had made it onto the ship. Nick had been briefed on the situation, along with all the others; he'd seen pictures. He knew it was a howler, and that he stood no chance against it unarmed. It was a long chilling moment before he could take his eyes off of it; the thing was eating Howard. It had thrust its head most of the way into his guts, chewing and slurping and swallowing loudly. Nick saw Howard lift his head, as if shaking off sleep, and look down at the grisly mess that used to be his torso. He moved his head slowly, to look at Nick.

His eyes were rusted red, and his flesh was a pale lifeless gray. He smiled sadly at

Nick, shook his head and looked back down at the monster. Lifting one hand, he laid it on the howler's head and pressed its hunger further into his bloody body cavity. With the other, he motioned toward the exit. Nick nodded, and moved. He threw one last look over his shoulder as he slipped through the egress; they were both lost in the feast, the monster's head still buried in flesh while his victim's eyes lolled ecstatically. Nick shuddered, and kept moving.

Sticking to the shorter passageways, Nick stayed alert for sounds while going over the briefing in his mind. Howard would be a rambler now, unless he got eaten entirely; he would be overwhelmed with a hunger for flesh, moving slowly and mindlessly. If he found it, and fed, he would begin another transformation. His slow movements would become unnaturally fast, the kind of speed displayed by predatory carnivores in the wild. The muscled arms that used to belong to Howard would lengthen, as would his legs; long sharp talons would sprout from his elongated fingers. The talons wouldn't turn someone, if he scratched them; but they were long enough and strong enough to be fatal. In the briefing, they had compared them to small swords, or long knives.

It was the bite that caused the change, both times. First you got bitten, then you bit someone else. Nick was determined to make it off the ship without being bitten or doing any biting; he racked his brain for ways he might accomplish the unlikely mission. He wished that he'd been on the ship longer; other than a brief tour, conducted by Howard back before he became something else, Nick knew nothing about the vessel. He'd had a weekend off between assignments, and he had spent it exploring yet another country that he had never been to; other than the location of his bunk, and one person's first name, the ship was completely new to him. He couldn't even remember where he had boarded, or how to get back; he pressed on, heading upward and toward what he thought was the aft deck whenever the monsters and layout would allow.

They were everywhere, in every space that had anyone in it. Nick had hoped to find that he had time to alert others; all the others he saw were feasting or being feasted on. He avoided occupied rooms and passageways, even when it meant going up or turning around; without some serious firepower, he had no chance against one of those things. It wasn't long before he felt lost, and began to get scared; he heard his heart pounding harder than it should be in his chest, and felt sweat on his forehead. There was no need for it, other than the gruesome scenes he stumbled upon as he searched.

Nick tried to calm himself, to keep the smell of his fear from drawing one of them. The floor moved slightly under him, and for a moment he thought he was wobbling on his feet. His heart picked up its pounding again as he realized that he was wrong; the ship was moving. They had left port. Even if he found a boarding area, or even a cargo plank, it would lead to locked steel or deep green ocean. Nick sighed.

He knew where he had to go.

* * *

He had been heading the wrong way; the motion under his feet told him so, and Nick doubled back. The slight pull of the floor told him which way was aft; he drifted down and back as he had earlier moved upward and forward. Many of the same chambers and hallways he had passed through earlier were still empty; he found alternate routes to the ones that were quickly. Nick was learning the mind of the ship, the layout of its circulatory system; once he understood how it thought, or how its maker had, he moved easily in the directions he wanted to go. It still took awhile; the vessel was the largest he had been stationed on, a floating city with enough troops and arms to take over another.

Soon enough, he reached the engine room, or one of them; he pulled open the heavy door, slipped inside and pulled it shut behind him. He'd been sleeping in boxers and a tank top, with knee high socks bunched around his ankles. They were all drenched in sweat by the time he secured the door. It was hot in here, like he had known it would be. The temperatures would consistently run higher than the surface of his skin, and they wouldn't see his heat signature even if they came looking.

Nick thought it was a brilliant plan, right up until he tried to find a comfortable place to cubby himself in. It was all hard surfaces, some of them vibrating constantly; the noise was deafening, and interminable, and the heat was drawing moisture out through his skin at an alarming rate. There was a trail of wet circles on the floor where he had walked, and a dark puddle forming at his feet where he stood. The droplets were fading, evaporating in the order that they had dripped from his body or clothes; near the door, they had faded entirely.

With the sound of the engines roaring in his ears, Nick tried to go over what else he remembered about the zombies that had fed. They should be asleep during daylight hours; they would likely go into the heart of the ship and pile on top of each other in the morning, and lay in a tangled unconscious heap until night began to fall. That would be when he would want to go get water and food; mostly water. Trouble was, he didn't have an electronic device telling him what time it was. There was no daylight in the powerful bowels of the engine room, and there were no clocks on the walls. He had been awakened in another interior room, after sleeping an indeterminate amount of time; and he didn't know when he had dozed off to begin with.

Nick assumed there was still some time before he should make his move; even if they were monsters, they still had the minds of military men and women. They would secure the ship as well as they could before leaving themselves at all defenseless, and they would have daylight shifts no matter how hard it was to work them. The last tendrils of sleep had released his mind long ago, but Nick was still exhausted. He found a place that he could wedge himself, half sitting and half lying down. He would be obscured from view if anyone entered, and the loud sounds and smells of the busy room would hopefully hide any that he put off. He closed his eyes, trying to feel the pull of sleep again.

Sweat dripped from his body, the engine thrummed its unending rhythm in his ears, and it was hard to tell if he drifted off or not. The heat and the noise transformed the little metal room into a sweat lodge, and psychedelic visions competed with ordinary thoughts for what little space remained in Nick's pounding head. He even dreamed, or imagined, that a howler entered the room while he lay there in awkwardly pained exhaustion. He opened his eyes to see it watching him, standing in the doorway; he watched it move closer, sniff at him and shake its head; he watched it move away, and close the door behind it. His pulse pounded through the vision, while Nick lay there motionless; after, he dismissed the hazy memory as a drifting dream.

When the ship slowed, he didn't notice. The engine changed pitch, but the sound was still hard and loud and thrumming; his ears had created the effect of a change in pitch several times as they endured the constant punishment, and Nick couldn't tell the difference. Even when the engine began winding down, and came to a slow rolling stop, he wasn't sure what was happening. It wasn't until the temperature began to drop that he realized they had stopped; when he stood, Nick nearly blacked out. He teetered toward the door, trembling and wobbling, and leaned his weight against it. There was no puddle at his feet, and his clothes were beginning to dry on his thirsty skin.

Nick licked his lips; it was like sandpaper on wood, rough and dry. He blinked, trying to clear his vision, and worked the handle with both hands. When the door came open at last, he leaned against it for another full minute. He was panting, and would have been sweating if he'd had it in him. The only reason he finally moved was the sense of urgency he was feeling. Nick needed to get to some water, and a little food, and maybe find a better hiding spot.

Dropping mental breadcrumbs, he moved up the hallway cautiously. There were no sounds for him to hear, even if his ears weren't ringing loudly already. Poking his head into doorways and pressing his face to thick windows showed nothing but rooms devoid of occupants. The sleeping quarters looked more appealing than he ever knew they could, but he couldn't afford to assume the ship was entirely empty yet. Perhaps they had docked, and were flooding some city; or maybe they were just drifting, and sleeping off whatever hangovers zombies got from frenzied feeding. Nick moved carefully, his hearing coming back to him bit by bit, until he found the galley.

The kitchens weren't locked down like the weapons caches. Nick went through the door and pounced on the nearest water cooler. He put his face under it and drank, choking and gasping and drinking more all the while. The water ran in rivulets down his face, soaking his tank top and dripping a few cold droplets on his boxers. It was like a dream, and Nick wondered while he drank if he was still tripping hard in the engine room. He didn't care, and dismissed the thought; there was more water to gulp down. When he had finally had his fill, Nick's belly was round with liquid under his tank top. It sloshed around inside him as he walked, searching steel cabinets and cupboards for food.

When the floor lurched under his feet this time, Nick felt it. He also felt the blood drain from his face, and the breath whoosh from his lungs. He moved to the exit immediately, and stepped into the steel hallway. With a bottle of water under each arm, and a packet of rations in each hand, Nick made his way back the way he had come. He made it to the engine room without encountering any of them, and breathed his first real breath in minutes as he closed the door behind him.

The sound was deafening, palpable, painful; it seemed louder than before. Rather than get used to it, his ears seemed to have grown more sensitive to the pounding thrum. Nick turned to face the sound, as bravely as he could, and dropped the bottles and bags at his feet.

It hadn't been a dream. It was the same monster, the one that had approached Nick and sniffed at him while he danced with delirium. The horrific hallucination had been real, and now it was back. Nick backed against the door, stopped when his feet began to skid under him.

"Please," he said, quietly.

The sound was lost in the thunderous pounding of the giant engine.

Nick took a deep breath, to raise his

voice, then thought better of it; he didn't want to make any aggressive moves, or sounds that might give that impression. He listened to his heart, keeping intense time with the overwhelming sound. He watched the monster, kept still, and waited.

While he watched, Nick realized that he knew this monster, or had before the change had taken him. His fatigues were soaked in his own blood, and layered over with those of countless others, but his features were hauntingly familiar. The harsh lines of his skull had changed, but not completely.

"Howard..." Nick murmured.

He didn't even hear his own voice, but the monster perked up. It nodded, and began to move toward him. Nick pressed himself against the door more insistently, and his heart began to pound faster than the engine could cycle. It stopped short of him, went down on all fours and sniffed at the rations. Nick could have sworn there was sadness in his rusted red eyes when he stood again. Howard shouldered him aside, easily threw the handle and swung wide the heavy door. Without looking at him again, the monster stepped through the door and closed it behind him.

Nick sighed, and fear and air whooshed

out together. He bent to pick up the food and water, straightened and went back to his cubby.

Suddenly, the sound didn't seem so bad.

* * *

The next time the ship stopped, Nick was ready. Blocking out the sound, and the heat, he retraced his steps in his mind while he waited. When the engine began to wind down, he moved. He found his way to the bunk he had been assigned, and opened the locker. He considered donning fatigues for a moment, and then decided on his street clothes. Camouflage wasn't going to disguise him from troops that hunted by smell and sound and heat, and there was no navy left to belong to anymore. Jeans and a buttoned shirt seemed as good of an outfit as any to face the apocalypse in. He tied his boots quickly, and explored passageways strategically until he found what he was looking for.

A huge chunk of steel had been slid aside at the end of the corridor, and he could see daylight beyond. He moved along the wall, cautious but quick, until he was looking out over the ocean. The water was a good ten or fifteen feet below, and most of the view was blocked by the other vessel. It was a cruise ship, stopped in its path to drift beside the military behemoth. There were howlers climbing all over the hull, skittering across the metal with chilling speed. They were leaping into the water as well, and swimming. Nick realized that they had finished with the other vessel already, and were swimming back toward the ship. One began to climb the hull under him, stabbing the metal with its talons and hefting itself from the water.

Nick backed away from the opening, and bumped into something that hadn't been there before. He turned, startled, and caught his own frightened cry before it escaped his lips.

"Howard," he sighed, gasping for air and listening to the pounding of his heart in his chest. It felt like the engine was still battering his body, pulsing sound at him with the maddening repetition of endless small blows. Nick felt his head start to spiral, and his vision began to go dark; Howard caught him as he fell, and carried him into a storage room nearby. His head was clearing as Howard set him down, gently as a monster could, and Nick protested.

"I need to go back to the engine room," he whispered fiercely. "They'll see me in here."

Howard cocked his head to the side, and looked at him curiously.

"My heat signature," Nick said quietly.

The creature's eyes went wide, and he shook his head. He rapped his gnarled fist on the metal wall above Nick lightly.

"What?" Nick frowned. "You can't see it through metal?"

Howard nodded.

"You can talk, can't you?" Nick was still frowning.

When Howard matched his expression, sharp jagged rows of teeth showed between what used to be his lips. Another look of great sadness spread across what used to be his face. He growled, quietly, and shook his head. Then he spoke; a chill ran up Nick's spine when he did, and it was all he could do to keep from shuddering.

"My voice," Howard said, wincing at the harsh graveled sound of it. "I sound like a monster."

It was hard to pull the words from the soup of sound that had been Howard speaking. Nick finally figured it out, and shrugged helplessly.

"I'm sorry," he said.

Howard nodded, and spoke again.

"Me too," he growled.

He turned his back, and moved for the door.

"I have to get off this ship," Nick said softly.

Howard stopped, but he didn't turn.

"I know," he grumbled. "Not here; it's too late. I will help. Wait here."

Nick opened his mouth to thank him, but the door was already coming open. He crumpled further against the wall, and waited. A few days ago he may have found himself annoyed to be in a small space awaiting orders; it was one of the few things he disliked about serving, the waiting. Now he was glad to wait, to have a flat surface to spread out on and a quiet rhythmic hum to put him at ease. It didn't matter that the hum was the distant sound of the engines; he didn't have the fear of having to return there any more, and it was soothing enough to lull him into the sleep he needed so badly. Howard nudged him when he returned, and Nick had to fight off his initial reaction to having woke up with a monster.

"Hey," he said, rising to his feet. "Are we stopping?"

Howard nodded. "Not now, but soon."

His voice was clearer, or Nick was getting used to it. There was something else, though; something was different.

"Did you get bigger?" Nick asked.

He had been taller than Howard when they'd met, and broader about the shoulders; now the monster had a good three inches on him.

Howard nodded again. He looked away.

"I fed," he growled. "The more we eat, the bigger we get."

"Did we stop while I was sleeping?"

Howard shook his head, met his eyes.

"We are capturing large groups, especially the ones we encounter by daylight. If we have enough food already, we often sink them instead of boarding," he explained. "At night we feast, and hunt drifting vessels for the pleasure of it; day raids are quick and surgical strikes. The boarding party eats only what it needs, and puts the rest in the brig."

Howard saw his eyes go wide, and he shook his head.

"You can't save them," he said. "Not from them, not from me."

Nick sighed, and nodded.

"Night is falling," Howard mused. "I can feel it."

He gave Nick a sideways glance that chilled his blood, then moved to the door.

"It's a small vessel," Howard said. "Your

best bet is to jump out and swim to the back of the boat, wait for us to leave."

Nick nodded. He moved to the door as it swung open. His hand fell on Howard's shoulder. It was hard as rock, wet with the blood that stood out in the ridges between sinew. Howard turned, met Nick's eyes.

"Thank you, Howard," he said. "Thank God for you."

"This wasn't God," Howard said, stiffening. "It was nature."

Nick opened his mouth, to ask what he meant; Howard brushed his hand aside, nudged him into the hallway. With a speed that Nick could barely see, he moved to the wide sliding door and opened it. There were footsteps in the hallway, and low howls resounding through the corridor. Howard grasped him roughly by the arm. Before he could thank him again, or take a breath, Nick was flying through the opening and falling toward the water.

Twisting to see what he could, Nick caught a glimpse of the other vessel before he struck the sea. He lifted his head from the water briefly, to suck in as much air as he could, then dove deep and stroked toward the glimpse. It wasn't far off, and had been tiny compared to the sailing city of destruction. Nonetheless, it had looked like the kind of vessel that very few could afford, a fully contained yacht nicer than the average home. Nick swam under it, running his hand along the smooth bottom until it ended. He popped his head up behind the boat, grasped the ladder with one hand and floated there, listening.

He heard a woman's voice, shouting from the deck of the yacht.

"Hey!" she cried out. "You're headed right for us! Divert your course or state your reasons for approaching!"

Nick realized he was trembling, from the cold or the frightened anticipation of knowing what was about to happen. He held the ladder, feeling like a coward as he heard a scream split the air. Gunshots followed, and another wretched scream; Nick trembled and held onto the ladder, salty tears coursing from his eyes to the sea. He had been trained for battle, but not for hopelessness.

Even when he knew they were dead, and the shots and screams stopped, Nick had to fight the urge to climb the ladder and throw himself at the murderous monsters. Something inside of him held him there, insisting that he live to fight another day. Even with the world falling apart, there was a mission left somewhere for him to complete. If it was a suicidal one, it would be because lives were saved when his was lost. Fighting now would be giving up hope, and hope was all he had. He listened to the engines firing up, the howls fading into the night as the sun set over the water. He climbed the ladder, still trembling, and pulled himself up on deck.

There were three bodies on deck, and a great deal of blood; it was splashed about in droplets and bursts, and puddled up in several places. Nick rolled the first corpse to the side, and pushed it into the water. It had been a howler; he smiled for the first time in what felt like forever as he turned the next one over; it was a howler as well. He dragged it across the deck, rolled it over the side, and went to the last body. The light was fading, and his chest was heaving with his efforts, when Nick paused at the last body. Standing over it, he felt his smile fade.

Nick knelt slowly, put his hand on the corpse's shoulder.

"Thank you, Howard," he said, quietly.

There was a pistol lying next to him, with a bit of blood on the barrel. Nick picked it up, tucked it in his waistband, and smiled again.

"I think we would have been friends," he said, "if the world hadn't done this to you. I don't know why you saved me, but I promise that I won't waste this opportunity. I'll find a way to help someone, like you did me, or I'll die trying."

He bit his lip, so he wouldn't cry.

"Like you did," he murmured.

Letting his hand fall from Howard's shoulder to his arm, Nick grasped his sleeve and dragged him over the smooth flooring. A wide streak of red followed them to the edge, and Nick pushed him into the sea. He watched the corpse hit the water, and sink swiftly out of sight.

It was nearly full night. The sun was gone, as was the fading last light of its setting. Nick trudged to the cabin, opened the door and stepped inside. It was the opposite of what he had witnessed on deck, calm clean lines describing a stateroom that looked like a living room and a galley that looked like a fully appointed kitchen. The quiet stillness of being alone and safe overwhelmed him for a moment. Nick stood there, looking at the shockingly normal scene, until his belly rumbled.

He went to the sink, tasted the water and then drank his fill from the faucet. The fridge was right there, and full-sized, and he almost cried when he opened it. It was stocked full of fresh food, good food, the kind of food that one prepared carefully before eating it. It was much better than what he ate even when he was home; compared to the rations that had filled his belly of late, it was almost too much.

Almost. Nick nibbled on a slice of cheese while he pulled out all of the ingredients he would need to make a proper breakfast. He closed the refrigerator door, holding an armful of food, and turned to place it on the counter. Movement from the corner of his eye made him jump, and drop the food; then she started screaming, and he spread his hands defenselessly.

"It's okay," Nick said. "I'm not going to hurt you. I only-"

She screamed again, her voice rising in pitch and volume to a painful level. Nick clapped his hands over his already pummeled ears.

"Please stop screaming!" he cried. "I'm not going to hurt you!"

It looked like she was getting ready to scream again; Nick stepped over the fallen packages at his feet as she gasped in a lungful of air. Her eyes went wide suddenly, then rolled back in her head. Nick moved forward more quickly, and caught her as she fell. He lifted her, and carried her in his arms, speaking quietly to her.

"I'm going to lay you down," he told her. "You need to calm down. I'm not going to hurt you. My name's Nick. Let's get you settled now, that's it. Just relax. There's nothing to worry about any more. You'll feel all better in a minute, then we'll talk. I'm going to go get you some water, okay?"

His head was reeling as he went into the galley once more. He called out comforting words to her while fetching a glass and filling it with water. He tried to hide how bad he felt for her; she was so young, and must have just lost her family right before her eyes. He said a quiet prayer of thanks, to God or Howard or nature, for bringing them together. Then he went back into the bedroom, carrying the water and speaking more calming words to her.

All was right with his world; Nick had a mission.

Dear Reader,

Wasn't that great? Isn't Nick such a cool guy? Let me tell you now what that shift was, and why it made me so happy to see it happen. When I outlined these stories, everything was pretty well laid out on this one. As much as I loved the story, I couldn't find a portal to see through the eyes that the outline had called for.

This was set up as a monster story, told through the perspective of the howler that saves Nick. Well, Howard wasn't having any of it. He liked Nick even more than I did, but he didn't want to tell me much; when I thought about it, I saw why. This had to be Nick's story, for a whole host of reasons.

As much as it has been part of the point of all this to see the world through the eyes of the proverbial monster, the overall story is more about people than zombies. This was one of those times when the story itself had to remind me of that, and show me how to tell this part. None of the action changed, but the different perspective was able to shine a light on things much more effectively.

If you loved these stories, and I hope you did, I would sincerely appreciate a review on Amazon.com or Goodreads.com.

Reviews help bring authors and readers together, uniting folks of like mind and complementary desires. If you'd like some help with writing reviews, I posted a tutorial on JayNorry.com to guide readers through what should be an enjoyable experience.

If you don't want to leave a review, I'm still very glad that you read this book. You're helping my dream come true just by doing that, and I'm grateful to you for your participation. Speaking of participation...

There is something else you can do if you liked these stories, and especially if you liked the commentary. You can join my newsletter, free of charge, and get access to all kinds of bonus content that is only for subscribers. I'll send you a weekly update, letting you know what's going on with me and the books, and you will become a member of the 'Secret Society of Deeper Meaning'! Not to brag, but it is my most favorite secret society ever.

One last time...I hope you loved the book! I say it because I mean it, and the thought of you feeling satisfied as it winds to a close makes me feel all kinds of happy.

Thanks for reading!
All the best,
Jay
Jay@JayNorry.com

Also available from J.K. Norry. . .

<u>Zombie Zero</u>
Zombie Zero: The First Zombie
Zombie Zero: The Last Zombie (Oct 2016)

<u>Zombie Zero: The Short Stories</u>
Volume 1: The Sickness Spreads
Volume 2: The Beginning of the End
Volume 3: Love Lost at Sea
Volume 4: The Zombie Killers (Oct 2016)
Volume 5: Monstrous Consequences (Nov 2016)
Volume 6: The Heart of the Monster (Dec 2016)

<u>The Walking Between Worlds trilogy</u>
Demons & Angels (Book I)
Rise of the Walker King (Book II)
Fall of the Walker King (Book III)

<u>As Jay Norry</u>
Stumbling Backasswards Into the Light

Learn more about the author at
<u>www.JayNorry.com</u>